# HISTORY ALIVE THROUGH MUSIC

## Musical Memories of

## Laura Ingalls Wilder

Written and Edited by

## William T. Anderson

Color Photography by

## Leslie A. Kelly

## HEAR & LEARN PUBLICATIONS

*This book is dedicated to Vivian Glover, for many years the pioneering spirit and devoted caretaker of the Laura Ingalls Wilder Memorial Society in De Smet, South Dakota.*

Cover: "In Search of the Land of Milk and Honey" by Harvey Dunn.
The original Dunn painting hangs in the Hazel L. Meyer Memorial Library, De Smet, South Dakota

ISBN 1-879459-08-6 (Book)
ISBN 1-879459-09-4 (Book and Tape Set)

Library of Congress Catalog Card Number 92-73046

Distributed by
Hear & Learn Publications
603 SE Morrison Road
Vancouver, Washington 98664
(206) 694-0034

Text ©1992 William T. Anderson
Color photography ©1992 Leslie A. Kelly
Musical Score © 1992 Hear & Learn Publications

Musical Memories of Laura Ingalls Wilder © 1992 Hear & Learn Publications
Printed in Korea for Terrell Publishing Co., Kansas City, Missouri

# able of Contents

## An Introduction

The Homestead Act of 1862 heralded the cry of "Free Land!" to an already footloose nation of pioneers. The lure of new opportunities, tracts of homestead land, adventures and better lives set into motion the last phase of America's pioneer movement. Within thirty years' time, most of the western United States had been settled, the frontier line pushed farther and farther toward the Pacific coast. Towns, railroads, telegraphs, settled farm country and Americans of all nationalities covered the broad lands west of the Mississippi River where previously only wild animals and Indians had roamed. By the early 1890s, historian Frederick Jackson Turner declared that the American frontier was indeed closed.

One family who along with thousands of others helped to settle the great American plains was that of Charles and Caroline Ingalls. With their four daughters Mary, Laura, Carrie and Grace, they were among the great waves of pioneers who headed west in search of new homes. Starting from their home in western Wisconsin in the late 1860s, this close-knit family spent a decade of covered wagon moves and brief settlements in four states before they finally established a permanent homestead. Their lives in Wisconsin, Kansas, Iowa, Minnesota and South Dakota were filled with hardships, dangers, achievements and the challenges of living close to the earth.

Sixty years later, the second daughter of the family, by then writer Laura Ingalls Wilder, began writing of her family's pioneering experiences in the now-classic *Little House* books. She wrote the truth of homesteading as she remembered it, never fictionalizing or glamorizing in her warm-hearted plain prose style. Publishing her first book at the age of sixty-five in 1932, Laura continued her literary work for eleven years, retiring from writing at the age of seventy six. She had penned eight books.

Laura wrote from her home-base of Rocky Ridge Farm near Mansfield, Missouri. She settled on that farm with her husband, Almanzo, in 1894, following her girlhood of pioneering. To that farm came a rich harvest of honors and recognition as the world paid her tribute as the author of the *Little House* books. When she died in February, 1957, just three days after her ninetieth birthday, Laura Ingalls Wilder knew that she had left behind as her legacy an enduring, classic story of America and its pioneers.

The Little House books include: *Little House in the Big Woods, Farmer Boy, Little House on the Prairie, On the Banks of Plum Creek, By the Shores of Silver Lake, The Long Winter, Little Town on the Prairie, These Happy Golden Years* and *The First Four Years.*

Of the rigors of pioneering, Laura wrote that "Everything came at us out of the west...storms, blizzards, grasshoppers, burning hot winds and fire...yet it seemed that we wanted nothing so much as we wanted to keep on going west." Family life for the Ingalls family was often bare of comforts and luxuries, but rich in hope, plans and security. Charles and Caroline Ingalls provided a sense of home and togetherness that was unshakeable.

One of Laura Ingalls Wilder's deepest satisfactions in the writing of her books was the knowledge that she could preserve the memory of her pioneering father. "He was always jolly, inclined to be reckless and loved his violin," she remembered.

"Pa's fiddle" was so much a part of the *Little House* books that it was almost a character in those stories. Like most fiddlers of his time, Pa Ingalls was probably self-taught as a musician. No one in the family thought to ask him how he acquired his fiddle on the frontier of Wisconsin, but even as a young man he was often called upon to play for neighborhood dances. On each move west, the fiddle was carefully packed among the quilts for safe-keeping. But it was as near as Pa's gun, and a part of the evening's activities in each of the family's stopping places, whether along the western trail, in log cabins, dugouts, claim shanties or little towns all over the west.

"When the day's work was done, we sat in the twilight or by the evening lamp and listened to Pa's stories and the music of his violin, " Laura recalled. "Our little family must be self-sufficient for its own entertainment."

Pa was a versatile musician. He could sing in harmony with his own fiddling, or inspire the family during dark times to raise their voices together. On Sundays he was a one-man hymn-sing when the family was far from a church. At dances, his fiddling could rouse the dancers to jig and reel and square dance. The fiddle could wail and moan with the wind or drown out blizzard sounds with songs of cheer and courage. It could duet with whippoorwills or serenade the stars.

"Whatever religion, romance and patriotism I have," said Laura Ingalls Wilder, "I owe largely to the violin and Pa playing in the twilight."

The songs Pa played and the words sung by Laura and her family spoke of love and loss, praise to God, good times in the past and better times in the future. They instilled courage and faith, good humor and endurance. All of the songs familiar to Laura Ingalls Wilder in her youth have now become the *Musical Memories of Laura Ingalls Wilder.*

*Rocky Ridge Farm near Mansfield, Missouri was the home of Laura and Almanzo Wilder from the time they settled there in 1894 until their deaths. After a productive farming career, the Wilders lived quietly in this country setting while Laura produced her beloved **Little House** books. All of the books were written on this farm over an eleven year period (1932-1943). The house is now preserved as a memorial to the author and her family.*

#  Wait for the Wagon

"I was born in the Little House in the Big Woods of Wisconsin. From there, with my parents and sisters, I traveled in a prairie schooner across Minnesota, Iowa, Missouri, and Kansas, and into Indian Territory, where we lived in the Little House on the Prairie. Then travelling back to western Minnesota we lived for several years on the banks of Plum Creek. From there we went West again, to the shores of Silver Lake in Dakota Territory. We lived in De Smet, the Little Town on the Prairie, and I married Almanzo of *Farmer Boy,* just as I told in *These Happy Golden Years.*"

"Wait for the Wagon" is almost a theme song for the Ingalls family. Imagine, loading all the family owned in the canvas covered wagon, and heading into the uncertain frontier! But family love provided security, and home was home, whether it was the covered wagon, the camp-site on the lonesome land or cabins or shanties on the prairies.

When they settled near a town, as they did in Walnut Grove, Minnesota, the Ingalls family took advantage of social life, school and church. *On the Banks of Plum Creek* tells of the wagon ride to town on the Sunday when Laura first attended church. Pa was gleeful on the sunny Sunday morning, and sang the tune to "Wait for the Wagon."

Ma, always mindful of manners and appearances, thought they might better sing a Sunday morning hymn. So the mood was changed with her own favorite song, "There is a Happy Land, Far, Far Away."

*Some of Laura's Sunday School records and awards from Walnut Grove, Minnesota, are now on display at the Laura Ingalls Wilder Home and Museum in Mansfield, Missouri.*

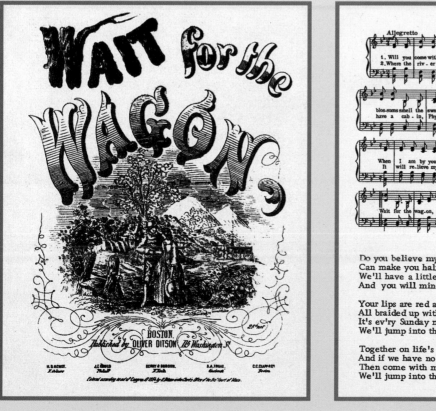

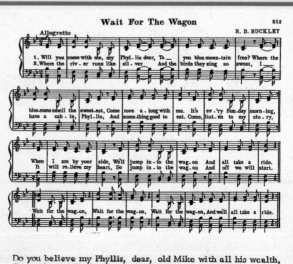

Do you believe my Phyllis, dear, old Mike with all his wealth,
Can make you half so happy, as I with youth and health!
We'll have a little farm--a horse, a pig and cow,
And you will mind the dairy, while I do guide the plow.

Your lips are red as poppies, your hair so slick and neat,
All braided up with dahlias, and hollyhocks so sweet;
It's ev'ry Sunday morning, when I am by your side,
We'll jump into the wagon and all take a ride.

Together on life's journey, we'll travel till we stop,
And if we have no trouble, we'll reach the happy top;
Then come with me, sweet Phyllis, my dear, my lovely bride,
We'll jump into the wagon, and all take a ride.

*When the Ingalls family left their home in the woods of Wisconsin, they left behind parents, brothers, sisters, cousins, and friends. Going west always had a sense of finality; no one knew whether they would see the travelers again. The first pioneering journey of the Ingalls family took them to Kansas, when they settled on the prairie near Independence. The site of **Little House on the Prairie** is now marked with this replica cabin.*

# reen Grows the Laurel

Partings...what pioneer did not feel that keen sense of separation? Infant deaths, unforeseen accidents, life-threatening weather and a battery of now-curable illnesses made the frontiersman of the 1800s value each new day.

The Ingalls family knew of partings, both permanent and temporary. Laura, for instance, never saw her grandparents after she left the Big Woods of Wisconsin. And anyone who has read the *Little House* books knows how longingly the Ingalls family wished for Pa's return when he traveled to town or worked in the wheat fields of eastern Minnesota.

Many of the songs Pa played with his fiddle were songs of parting, songs of love for the absent sweetheart and songs expressing joy on the return. The Civil War provided many such lyrics, and they carried over very meaningfully to the next decade when so many Americans left home to pioneer in the West.

On the evening before Pa left for his trading trip to Independence, Kansas (described in *Little House on the Prairie*), he sang these words to Ma:

> *So green grows the laurel,*
> *And so does the rue,*
> *So woeful, my love,*
> *At the parting with you.*

LAURA INGALLS WILDER HOME ASSOCIATION, MANSFIELD, MISSOURI

*Charles and Caroline Ingalls, soon after their wedding in 1860.*

9

*A steam engine uses a rotary snow plow to clear the railroad tracks in the big cut east of De Smet, South Dakota, 1896.*

# The Old Chariot
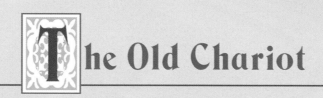

The railroad tracks were as much a part of the settling of the West as the homesteaders were. When new lands were open for settlement, railroad companies quickly planned and built extensions of their tracks. Where farming was established, there must also be the means to ship crops to markets.

The building of the Chicago and Northwestern Railroad into Dakota Territory in 1879 brought the Ingalls family to the area that became the town of De Smet. Pa worked as a timekeeper and paymaster as the railroad construction camps moved west. When the camp reached Silver Lake, the Ingalls family moved no farther west. They were present as the first family of the town when De Smet was estab-

lished in 1880. Laura tells of these times in *By the Shores of Silver Lake.*

After the early autumn blizzards of 1880, described in *The Long Winter,* Pa Ingalls was one of the men of De Smet who traveled by handcar to help clear the drifted railroad line. They journeyed thirty miles east to the town of Volga, stopping to shovel out the snow-clogged tracks.

Pa was always a leader in community spirit. He knew that work moves faster, and seems easier, when there was music. So he started the men in singing "The Old Chariot" all the way to Volga. Singing and shoveling, the men worked their way across the snowy prairies of Dakota Territory.

*A scene from De Smet's annual Laura Ingalls Wilder pageant.*

# 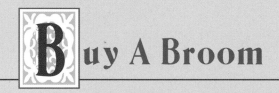uy A Broom

Like Pa, Laura discovered that singing made work go faster. When the Ingalls family settled briefly in the railroad camp along Silver Lake in Dakota Territory, it became Laura's duty to milk the cow. She joined her cousin Lena at the task, and the two girls sang together. Laura especially enjoyed the songs with waltz tempo. "Buy a Broom" was one of them.

Laura claimed that the singing she and Lena did during milking time encouraged the cows to let down their milk more easily. Later, dairy research proved that music in the cow barn did indeed encourage the milk to flow!

Laura, in her later life, claimed that she was never much of a singer, but she admitted that "there is always a little music in my feet." She loved to dance, and her record collection on Rocky Ridge Farm in Mansfield included recordings ranging from the classics to the old tunes she had known as a girl. Her old fashioned pump organ held many song-books which helped her reference lyrics when she was writing the *Little House* books.

*The Wilder's Electrola brought them hours of pleasure on Rocky Ridge Farm in Mansfield, Missouri.*

*By the Shores of Silver Lake* describes the winter of 1879-1880, when the Ingalls family lived many miles from any neighbor on the Dakota prairie.  Their home, the Surveyors' House, is now preserved by the Laura Ingalls Wilder Memorial Society of De Smet.

# weet By and By

Pa's favorite hymn, "The Sweet By and By", was a song of hope for better times and future promises.  Surely the Ingalls family knew the sense of longing for happier times. They waited patiently for good crops, the ending of long winters, the return of loved ones and prosperity which always seemed to elude them.  To them, "the beautiful" of this song meant all the things they hoped for.

When they were snowbound or miles from a church, the Ingalls family held their own Sunday School services.  "The Sweet By and By" was often a part of the music they sang. When Pa died in 1902, this song was sung at his funeral in the Congregational Church in De Smet which he helped to organize.

As Laura heard the words sung at Pa's funeral, she thought to herself that when her time came to die, she would like Pa's voice and the fiddle's strains to be playing that very song just for her.

*Pa Ingalls, 1890s*

*"I Am the Resurrection and the Life" by Harvey Dunn, portrays a prairie funeral during homestead years.*

*Pa and Ma's bedroom in the Ingalls home in De Smet*

# Rock Me To Sleep

Motherhood on the frontier was an especially noble calling; making a home and caring for a family carried many unforeseen challenges. The *Little House* books depict Laura's mother, Caroline Ingalls, as resourceful, courageous and serene through all manner of hardship.

"Although born on the frontier she was an educated, cultured woman," wrote Laura Ingalls Wilder of "Ma". "She was very quiet and gentle, but proud and particular in all matters of good breeding."

Reflecting on her mother's nurturing influence, Laura wrote: "The older we grow the more precious become the recollection of childhood's days, especially our memories of mother. Her love and care halo her memory with a brighter radiance, for we have discovered that nowhere else in the world is such loving self-sacrifice to be found; her counsels and instructions appeal to us with greater force than when we received them because our knowledge of the world and our experience of life have proved their worth."

"Rock me to Sleep", when performed at one of De Smet's "Literaries" in 1882, was a moving song. All the tender emotions associated with mothers seemed expressed in the song. Tears ran down the listeners' cheeks, and young Laura Ingalls was struck by the pathos of the song.

Who does not remember with affection being rocked to sleep in the loving arms of a mother?

*Caroline Ingalls, circa 1897*

*Laura Ingalls Wilder, 1890s*

*Laura Ingalls Wilder's birthplace near Pepin, Wisconsin is marked by the **"Little House Wayside"**. The original log cabin disappeared years before Laura became known as an author, but the present-day Laura Ingalls Wilder Memorial Society of Pepin maintains a replica.*

# uffalo Gals

"Buffalo Gals" was a popular toe-tapping tune familiar to Laura Ingalls and other Americans at dances and parties held at harvest time, at house-raisings, wedding dances or "sugaring-off" parties, like the one described in *Little House in the Big Woods*.

Pioneers often lived lives of isolation, but several times a year they managed to gather friends and family together for festivities like the "sugaring-off" which Laura remembered from the Wisconsin woods. On such occa-

sions, the tables groaned under the weight of delicious foods. Babies were lined up on the bed to sleep while their parents danced. Little children watched with awe as the adults danced until the early hours of the morning. Everyone, dressed in their finest, tried to outdo others in cookery, dancing style and the delicate art of boiling the maple sap until it was "just right". Poured over clean snow, the sap hardened into maple candy. The remainder was stored away as syrup and maple sugar.

# BUFFALO GALS

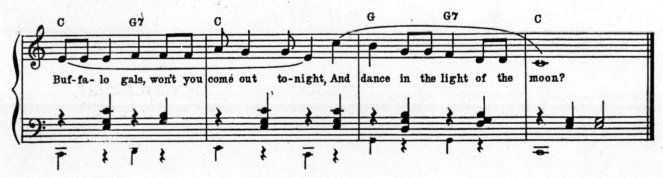

*The Dakota land boom of the 1880s was closely tied with the building of the Chicago and Northwestern Railroad through the Territory.*

# A Railroad Man For Me

"I understood that in my own life I represented a whole period of American history," wrote Laura Ingalls Wilder. She had seen the frontier, the farmer, the growth of towns, the building of railroads and the coming of the machine age. To her, writing the *Little House* books was a way to preserve a vanished era for American children.

In 1879, Laura was thrilled to watch the building of the railroad through Dakota Territory. The construction workers, in their striped shirts, working with powerful horses and machinery, seemed somehow exciting and curious to Laura and her cousin Lena. Lena sang "A Railroad Man for Me" with conviction. She said she'd much rather continue moving west with the railroads, rather than live the settled life of a farmer.

Laura spent most of her life as a farmer's daughter or a farmer's wife. She said of farming: "What's bred in the bone comes out in the flesh." The Ingalls family had always farmed, just as the Wilders had. Despite the glamour of railroading and the men who built the tracks, Laura was drawn to a farmer boy named Almanzo Wilder. Harvey Dunn's painting "Buffalo Bones are Plowed Under" depicts the Dakota farmer breaking sod to establish a prairie farm. Dunn (1884-1952), grew up within miles of the Ingalls homestead and became related to the family by marriage. His uncle Nate Dow married Laura's sister, Grace.

Laura heard Pa predict that one day railroads would take over as the prime transportation in America. He never envisioned the automobile, but Laura lived to drive in the Wilder Chrysler over the same prairie that she and her family had traversed by covered wagon.

Three times during the 1930s, Laura and Almanzo Wilder visited South Dakota, driving the distance from their home in Mansfield, Missouri. By then, covered wagons were only a memory and railroads were already on the wane. This picture shows Laura in the Badlands of South Dakota, with the car she and Almanzo drove in 1938.

*Almanzo Wilder came courting Laura Ingalls with his luxurious buggy and his Morgan horses. Together, they roamed across the prairies to Spirit Lake and to the Twin Lakes, Henry and Thompson. Their favorite month for buggy rides was June, when the prairies were covered with the fragrant blooms of the prairie rose. Later, Laura named her only daughter for those flowers which were so much a part of the Wilders' courting days.*

# Beware

When the Ingalls family moved to Dakota Territory in 1879, Laura was nearly thirteen and was as she described herself, a mix of child and adult. The rest of her youth was nurtured in and around De Smet. Growing up was often abrupt and demanding in pioneer times; Laura was just fifteen when she unexpectedly taught her first school.

Laura had learned the popular parlor song "Beware" from her cousin Lena. It told of betrayed love and insincere lovers. Whether or not she remembered the song when Almanzo Wilder came courting we do not know, but Laura was slow to warm to the handsome young homesteader who came calling with his fine horses. Ma wondered aloud if Laura liked the horses better than their master.

Almanzo courted Laura for three years. They were married in August of 1885. Longfellow's lyrics in "Beware", guarding against false sweethearts, had little to do with the loving trust established in the Wilder marriage. For sixty-four years, Almanzo and Laura Wilder were business partners, best friends and kindred spirits in a long and loving marriage.

*Laura and Almanzo Wilder, circa 1948*

*Pa's fiddle was kept by Laura in her Mansfield, Missouri home after her father's death in 1902.
In 1944, she gave the fiddle to the South Dakota State Historical Society in Pierre, where it was displayed
for many years. In 1962, it was transferred to the Laura Ingalls Wilder Home and Museum in
Mansfield, where it is currently on display. After many years of silence, the fiddle was played again,
in October of 1991, at a special program in honor of **Little House** illustrator Garth Williams.
The grounds surrounding Laura's home in the Ozarks resounded with the strains of
the historic fiddle, and "Pop! Goes the Weasel" was played again.*

# Pop! Goes The Weasel

The old American favorite, "Pop! Goes the Weasel", was a special tune which Pa played to his girls on occasions like their birthdays. On Laura's fifth birthday, February 7, 1872, Pa played this tune for his daughter. Pa liked to mystify the girls by popping the fiddle string so quickly that they could seldom see him do so as they sang "pop!"

Pa's fiddling was so much a part of her growing up years that Laura often associated cozy evenings by the firelight with her father's playing. In her daughter Rose's copy of *These Happy Golden Years,* Laura penned this verse:

*And so farewell to childhood days,*

*Their joys, and hopes and fears.*

*But Father's voice and his fiddle's song*

*Go echoing down the years.*

*The strains of Pa Ingalls' fiddle followed the pioneering lives of the Ingalls family through all their covered wagon journeys through America's heartland. Fond memories of the fiddle's song wind like a thread through the **Little House** books of Laura Ingalls Wilder. The original violin is now on exhibit at the Laura Ingalls Wilder Home and Museum in Mansfield, Missouri.*

*When the Ingalls family lived along Silver Lake during the winter of 1879-1880, they often placed the kerosene lamp in the window of the Surveyors' House, in case some lonely traveler chanced to see the light and needed shelter.*

# ft in the Stilly Night

"Oft in the Stilly Night" includes the line: "Fond mem'ry brings the light of other days around me." Memory prompted Laura Ingalls Wilder's writing of her *Little House* books. She said that her childhood recollections were "stories that had to be told" and that they were "altogether too good to be lost." Writing in pencil on lined yellow school tablets, she spun stories from her childhood that have been cherished since their publication.

"I have learned," she explained, "that when I went as far back in my memory as I could and left my mind there awhile it would go farther back and still farther, bringing out of the dimness of the past things that were beyond my ordinary remembrance."

Memories of home for Laura were often tied to memories of music. The winter the Ingalls family spent on Silver Lake in Dakota Territory was filled with winter evenings of song and fiddle music. When Mr. and Mrs. Robert Boast arrived to spend the winter, two new voices joined the Ingalls sing-a-longs. They sang their way through the "Pure Gold" hymn book, and often before bedtime, Pa would close with a slow, dreamy melody like "Oft in the Stilly Night." This tearful song spoke of long-departed friends and melancholy remembrance of them.

*The restored Surveyors' House in De Smet which was home to the Ingalls Family in 1879-1880.*

*"The Prairie is My Garden" by Harvey Dunn*

# The Girl I Left Behind Me

Pioneer women have never been given their just credit as gentle tamers of the West. Many women, both single and widowed, actually filed on homestead land, and most of them "proved up" on the claims. For those women who needed a career, homesteading was an option.

Eliza Jane Wilder, the sister of Almanzo, who was a character in both *Farmer Boy* and *Little Town on the Prairie,* was a "lady homesteader" during the early 1880s. She worked hard to farm her land near De Smet, battling bad weather, insects, illness and a general lack of knowledge in how to cope with prairie living. Perhaps worst of all was the isolation. "The utter silence and loneliness of the situation grew so terrible as to be unendurable and I think I fathomed the depth of the word *ALONE,*" wrote Eliza Jane.

Even married women like Caroline Ingalls and Laura Ingalls Wilder were faced with the prospect of running the family farm when their husbands were absent. Ma Ingalls bravely kept the Plum Creek farm going when Pa was absent, working in the East. Both Ma and Laura knew the long empty days on the empty prairies when their husbands were away.

Pioneer women were much like the wives and sweethearts left behind during the Civil War...when men fought battles with bravery and conviction.

THE ORIGINAL DUNN PAINTING HANGS IN THE HAZEL L. MEYER MEMORIAL LIBRARY, DE SMET, SOUTH DAKOTA

*Harvey Dunn caught the essence of the homesteading woman in this
painting "Pioneer Woman" now on exhibit in De Smet.*

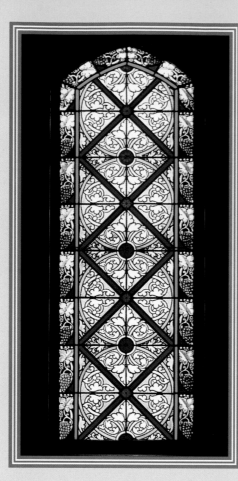

*Laura Ingalls Wilder attended both the Congregational and Methodist churches during her long lifetime. In 1890, she, her husband Almanzo and daughter Rose, lived for a year with Almanzo's parents on their farm near Spring Valley, Minnesota. While there, Laura attended services in the Methodist Church building, which was started in 1876. The church featured beautiful Italian stained glass windows which date to the 1700s. Laura worshipped along with the Wilders, who were important supporters of the church. Colors in the stained glass reflect eras in Laura's own long life: Green and yellow, for youth; red for maturity and experience; blue and purple for old age; and gold for eternal life. The latter is applicable and reflective of Laura's writing, which has timeless quality and enduring value.*

# 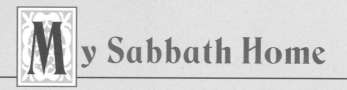 My Sabbath Home

Laura Ingalls Wilder grew up in a home where faith in God and His goodness were sustaining forces in daily life. Indeed, the Ingalls family endured its share of trials...grasshopper plagues that rivaled those of Bible times, poverty and illness, Mary's loss of eyesight, fire, flood, drought and isolation. But Ma was always quick to remind them to "never complain of what you have," to "thank Providence," and to "persevere."

Often the Ingalls family found themselves miles from any organized church. But Sunday was the Sabbath and they marked the day with good clothes, Bible stories and hymn singing. Whether alone on the prairie or isolated in the big woods, the Ingalls family respected Sunday as a day of rest and reverence.

When they were settled near frontier communities like Walnut Grove, Minnesota, Burr Oak, Iowa or De Smet, Dakota Territory, the Ingalls family was quick to join the local church and take a leading role in its development. Because of the activities of the Home Missionary Society of Boston, the Congregational church was active in the mid-west. Pa and Ma united with the Congregational denomination, and their girls attended Sunday School and church services with them.

Laura first joined the Sunday School class of the Union Congregational Church at Walnut Grove in 1874. There she heard and sang the words to "My Sabbath Home." It was a Sunday school song that followed her to Burr Oak in 1876 and back again to Walnut Grove in 1878 and finally out to De Smet in Dakota Territory in 1879. The first church services ever held in the De Smet vicinity were conducted at the Ingalls home along Silver Lake during the winter of 1880. Late that year, Pa and Ma helped to found the Congregational Church in De Smet.

Laura looked back with fondness on her girlhood memories of Sunday School...the memorization of Bible verses, the prize she won, the songs sung and the kindly, pious teachers who gave her religious training.

She mentions singing "My Sabbath Home" in both *On the Banks of Plum Creek* and *These Happy Golden Years*.

*The church bell Pa helped to buy still rings in the English Lutheran Church tower in Walnut Grove, Minnesota.*

*Laura's daughter Rose Wilder (standing second from left) participated in Sunday School exercises at the De Smet Congregational Church in June 1894.*

*Laura Ingalls Wilder in 1937*

# Musical Memories
## *of* Laura Ingalls Wilder

# Sheet Music
# Section

# Wait For The Wagon

Your lips are red as poppies,
Your hair so slick and neat,
All braided up with dahlias,
And hollyhocks so sweet.

It's ev'ry Sunday morning,
When I am by your side,
We'll jump into the wagon,
And all take a ride.

Together on life's journey,
We'll travel till we stop,
And if we have no trouble,
We'll reach the happy top.

Then come with me, sweet Phyllis,
My dear, my lovely bride,
We'll jump into the wagon,
And all take a ride.

# Green Grows The Laurel

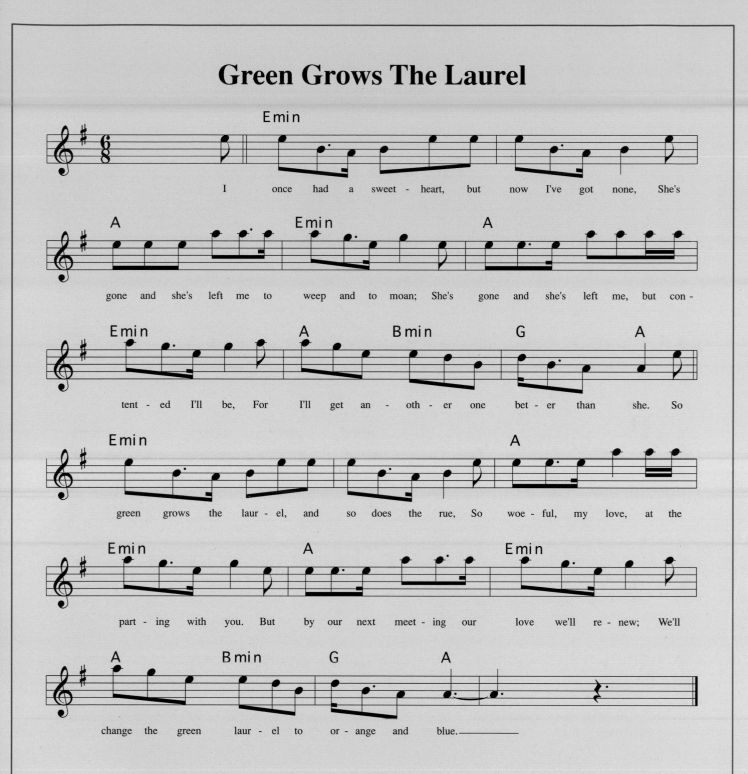

She wrote me a letter,
Four red rosy lines,
She wrote me another all twisted in twines;
Keep your love letter and I will keep mine,
And write to your sweetheart and I'll write to mine.

She passes my window both early and late,
The looks that she gives me,
They make my heart break,
The looks that she gives me a thousand times o'er,
You are the sweetheart I once did adore.

I oft times do wonder why young maids love men,
I oft times do wonder why young men love them;
But by my experience,
I now ought to know,
Young maids are deceivers wherever they go.

*CHORUS*
So green grows the laurel, and so does the rue,
So woeful, my love, at the parting with you.
But by our next meeting our love we'll renew;
We'll change the green laurel to orange and blue.

# The Old Chariot

We'll roll the old char - i - ot a - long we'll roll the old

char - i - ot a - long we'll roll the old char - i - ot a - long And we

won't drag on be - hind.
1. If the sin - ner's in the way, we will
2. If the Dev - il's in the way, we will

stop and take him in, if the sin - ner's in the way, we will
roll it o - ver him, if the Dev - il's in the way, we will

stop and take him in, If the sin - ner's in the way, we will
roll it o - ver him, If the Dev - il's in the way, we will

stop and take him in, And we won't drag on be - hind.
roll it o - ver him, And we won't drag on be - hind.

# Buy A Broom

To brush off the insects that come to annoy you
You'll find it quite useful by night and by day,
And what better exercise pray can employ you,
Than to sweep all vexatious intruders away?

*CHORUS*
Buy a broom, buy a broom!
Than to sweep all vexatious intruders away?

Ere winter comes on for sweet home soon departing.
My toils for your favor again I'll resume,
And while gratitude's tear in my eyelid is starting,
Bless a time that in England I cried buy a broom!

*CHORUS*
Buy a broom, buy a broom!
Bless a time that in England I cried buy a broom!

# Sweet By and By

We shall sing on that beautiful shore
The melodious songs of the blest,
And our spirits shall sorrow no more,
Not a sigh for the blessing of rest.

To our bountiful Father above,
We will offer the tribute of praise,
For the glorious gift of His love
And the blessings that hallow our days.

CHORUS
In the sweet by and by,
We shall meet on that beautiful shore;
In the sweet by and by,
We shall meet on that beautiful shore.

# Rock Me To Sleep

G                          D 7

Back - ward      turn   back - ward,      Oh   time   in   thy

G             C             G

flight,           Make    me   a    child    a - gain

G             D             D 7

just    for    to -   night.         Moth - er    come

G             D 7           G

back   from    the    ech -   o - less    shore.

D 7          G    Emin    C         D 7

Take    me   a -   gain    to    your    heart    as    of

G             D 7           G

yore;           Kiss   from   my    fore - head   the

fur - rows of care, Smooth the few

sil - ver threads out of my hair.

O - ver my slum - ber your lov - ing watch

keep; Rock me to sleep moth - er

rock me to sleep

Over my heart in days that are flown,
No love like mother love ever was shown;
No other worship abides and endures,
Faithful, unselfish, and patient like yours;
None like a mother can charm away pain
From the sick soul and the world weary brain.
Slumber's soft calm o'er my heavy lids creep;

Mother dear mother, the years have been long
Since I last hushed to your lullaby song;
Sing then and unto my soul it shall seem
Womanhood's years have been only a dream.
Clasped to your heart in a loving embrace,
With your light lashes just sweeping my face,
Never hereafter to wake or to weep;

*CHORUS*
Rock me to sleep,
Mother rock me to sleep!

# Buffalo Gals

I asked her if she'd have some talk,
Have some talk, have some talk,
Her feet took up the whole sidewalk
As she stood close by me.

I'd like to make that gal my wife,
Gal my wife, gal my wife,
I would be happy all my life
If I had her by my side.

*CHORUS*
Oh, you buffalo gals,
Will you come out tonight,
Come out tonight, come out tonight,
Buffalo gals won't you
Come out tonight
And dance by the light of the moon.

# A Railroad Man

C      F      C      F

I— would – n't mar – ry a farm – er, he's al – ways in the
I— would – n't mar – ry a black – smith, he's al – ways in the

G      C      F

dirt,    I'd rath – er mar – ry a rail – road man Who
black,    I'd rath – er mar – ry an en – gi – neer That

G7      C      C

wears a strip – ed shirt!    Oh, a rail – road man a
throws the throt – tle back! 

F      C      G7

rail – road man, A rail – road man for me!

C      C7      F

I'm going to mar – ry a rail – road man, A

C      G7      C

rail – road – er's bride——— I'll be!

# Beware

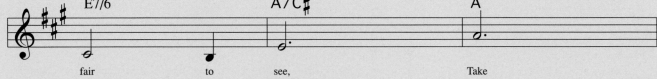

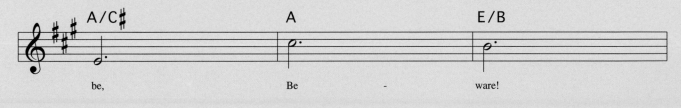

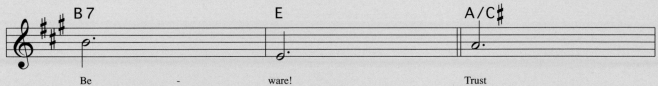

**C#dim**

*her*

**D**

*not,*

**Bmin**

*she's fool - ing*

**E**

*thee;*

**E7/6**

*she's fool - ing*

**A**

*thee*

**E7**

*Trust*

**A/C#**

*her*

**C#dim**

**D**

*not,*

**Bmin**

*she's fool - ing*

**A/E**

*thee she's*

**E7/6**

*fool - ing*

**A**

*thee.*

She has two eyes so soft and brown,
Take care! take care!
She gives a side glance and looks down,
Beware! beware!

And she has hair of golden hue,
And what she says, it is not true,

She gives a garland woven fair,
It is a fool's cap for to wear,

*CHORUS*
Trust her not, she's fooling thee;
She's fooling thee;
Trust her not, she's fooling thee;
She's fooling thee.

# Pop!  Goes The Weasel

# Oft in the Stilly Night

bro - ken.    Thus    in    the    still - y    night,    Ere
part - ed.

slum - ber's    chain    hath    bound——— me.    Sad    mem - 'ry

brings    the    light    of    oth - er    days    a - round    me.

# The Girl I Left Behind Me

The wind did blow,
The rain did flow,
The hail did fall
And blind me;
I thought of the girl,
The sweet little girl,
The girl I'd left behind me!
The sweet little girl,
The pretty little girl,
The girl I left behind me,
I thought of the girl,
The sweet little girl,
The girl I'd left behind me!

She wrote ahead the place I said,
A letter to remind me;
She says "I'm true;
When you get through
Ride back and you will find me."
The sweet little girl,
The pretty little girl,
The girl I left behind me,
She says, "I'm true;
When you get through
Ride back and you will find me."

If ever I get off the trail,
And the Indians they don't find me,
I'll make my way straight back again
To the girl I left behind me.
The sweet little girl,
The pretty little girl,
The girl I left behind me,
I'll make my way straight back again
To the girl I left behind me!

# Sabbath Home

1. Sweet Sab - bath school more dear to me Than
2. Here first my will - ful wan - d'ring heart The

fair - est pal - ace dome. My heart e'er turns with
way of life was shown. Here first I sought the

joy to thee, My own dear Sab - bath home. Sab - bath
bet - ter part, And gained a Sab - bath home.

home! Bles - sed home! Sab - bath Home! Bles - sed Home! My

heart e'er turns with joy to thee, My own dear Sab - bath Home.

## Musicians

*From left to right: (Standing) Diana Waring, John Standefer (Seated) Craig Russell, Tad Suckling.*

Tad Suckling owns and operates Cozy Dog Recording Studio in Vancouver, Washington, where he engineers and produces albums for a wide variety of musical groups. He is a singer and song writer in his own right beginning his career with Four Star Television in California. He is sought out by numerous recording groups familiar with his well-known musical expertise. He is a descendant of one of England's noted poets, Sir John Suckling, the creator of the card game Cribbage.

Craig Russell is an arranger and producer of albums as well as being an exceptional studio keyboard musician. He is also a music teacher of blind and visually impaired children. Craig is a wooden flute enthusiast and plays several wind instruments and is frequently in demand as a piano player for live performances.

John Standefer began playing guitar at age five and was teaching in a conservatory and playing professionally by age 15. He plays guitar, mandolin, banjo and various other stringed instruments. He performs concerts for school children in the Portland, Oregon, area as well as live jazz concerts and extensive studio work. Raised in a musical family, John's father was a fiddler and fiddle maker and his mother was a Kentucky hillbilly singer with her own radio show in the 30s and 40s.

Diana Waring is a folk singer with a wide range of interests and a writer specializing in American history. She is a homeschool mom whose interest in music and history led to the development of the Hear & Learn Publications' books and tapes. Her Grandfather, a fiddler, banjoist and story teller, was a trail driver on the Chisholm Trail.

Their previous books and tapes are: *America 1750-1890* (1990 Hear & Learn Publications) and *Westward Ho!* (1990 Hear & Learn Publications) which have received wide acceptance in the field of education. Those songs, and *Musical Memories of Laura Ingalls Wilder,* were recorded and edited at Cozy Dog Recording Studio in Vancouver, Washington.

## Author and Photographer

*From left to right: Leslie A. Kelly, Photographer, Garth Williams, Little House Books Illustrator, and William T. Anderson, Author, pose in front of Rocky Ridge Farm, Laura and Almanzo's home in the Ozarks at Mansfield, Missouri. It was here in this house that Laura first penned her adventures on the prairies of the pioneer Midwest in her now famous books on yellow pads purchased for a nickel apiece.*

William T. Anderson is the pre-eminent biographer of Laura Ingalls Wilder and her family. Some of his books include *Laura Ingalls Wilder: A Biography* (1992), *Laura Ingalls Wilder Country* (1990) and *A Little House Sampler* (1989), all published by HarperCollins. Earlier works include a series of biographical works on the Ingalls and Wilder families, including *The Story of the Ingalls and Laura Wilder of Mansfield,* and *Little House Country Photo Guide* (with Leslie A. Kelly). His work has also appeared in many magazines, including *The Saturday Evening Post, Travel and Leisure, American History Illustrated, Highlights for Children, Jack and Jill,* and *The Christian Science Monitor.* He is a frequent guest speaker on Ingalls-Wilder lore at conferences, universities, schools and libraries around the country.

Leslie A. Kelly is internationally known for his photography of the *Little House* sites which have appeared in *Little House On The Prairie Photo Guide* (Anderson and Kelly, 1988 Kyuryudo, in Japanese), *Little House Country Photo Guide* (Anderson and Kelly, 1989 Terrell), *A Rookie Biography: Laura Ingalls Wilder, Author of the Little House Books* (Greene, 1990 Childrens Press), *Laura Ingalls Wilder Country* (Anderson and Kelly, 1990 HarperCollins), *Laura Ingalls Wilder: A Biography* (Anderson, 1992 HarperCollins) and numerous magazine articles in the U.S., Europe and Japan. He is also credited with *America's Amish Country* (Yoder and Kelly, 1992 America's Amish Country Publications).

## PHOTO CREDITS

Leslie A. Kelly: 5, 6, 7, 8, 11, 12, 13, 14, 16, 18, 22, 24, 25, 26, 27, 30, 31 upper, 52 both • Laura Ingalls Wilder Home Association, Mansfield, Missouri: 9 • Laura Ingalls Wilder Memorial Society, De Smet, South Dakota: 17 • Hazel L. Meyer Memorial Library, De Smet, South Dakota: Cover, 29 • South Dakota Art Museum, Brookings: 15 lower, 21 upper, 28 • South Dakota State Historical Society, Pierre: 10, 20 • William T. Anderson Collection: 15 upper, 21 lower, 23, 31 • HarperCollins Publishers' Publicity Department: 32 • Page 12: Laura Ingalls Wilder Pageant, De Smet, South Dakota, used with permission. • Page 24: Herbie Johnston, Norwood, Missouri, playing Pa's fiddle October 12, 1991, used with permission. • Page 52 right: Picture of Leslie A. Kelly, Garth Williams and William T. Anderson taken by Philip Sadler.